For my mom; and for the Japanese
*rakugo* that always made me laugh

Copyright © 2019 Yuko Katakawa
All Rights Reserved
HOLIDAY HOUSE is registered in the U.S. Patent
and Trademark Office.
Printed and bound in November 2018 at Toppan Leefung,
DongGuan City, China.
The artwork was created with mixed media.
www.holidayhouse.com
First Edition
1 3 5 7 9 10 8 6 4 2
Library of Congress Cataloging-in-Publication Data
Names: Katakawa, Yuko, author, illustrator.
Title: Let's scare Bear / Yuko Katakawa.
Other titles: Let us scare Bear
Description: First edition. | New York : Holiday House, [2019]
Summary: Mouse, Fox, Snake, and Spider try to frighten Bear,
the biggest, loudest, bravest, strongest—and possibly
trickiest—animal in the forest.
Identifiers: LCCN 2018023829 | ISBN 9780823439539 (hardcover)
Subjects: | CYAC: Forest animals—Fiction. | Fear—Fiction.
Tricks—Fiction.
Classification: LCC PZ7.1.K372 Let 2019 | DDC [E]—dc23
LC record available at https://lccn.loc.gov/2018023829

# LET'S SCARE BEAR

## YUKO KATAKAWA

HOLIDAY HOUSE · NEW YORK

Manju cake!
Chewy! Sweet! A treat to eat!

Mouse loved manju.
Fox loved manju.
Spider loved manju.
And Snake loved manju too.

They were about to enjoy
their manju feast when . . .

they heard a THUMP

THUMP
THUMP.

Bear was passing by. Bear was the biggest, loudest, bravest, and strongest animal in the forest.

Mouse spoke with a teeny tiny voice,
and he wasn't brave or strong at all.

"Let's scare Bear," Mouse
squeaked to his friends.

"I'll go first," said Fox.

Fox flashed his knife-sharp teeth at Bear.

Bear flashed his knife-sharp teeth back at Fox and laughed.

Spider tried to trap Bear in a sticky web.

Bear broke it with
his powerful paw.

*help*

Snake wrapped her
strong coils around Bear.

But Bear burst right through.

Little Mouse tried to say

But only a tiny "squeak" came out.

Bear laughed again.

"Only one thing scares me," said Bear.

The others waited breathlessly.

"Manju cake," said Bear.

"Manju cake?" asked Mouse.

Bear began to shiver and quiver,
quake and shake.
All at the thought of
MANJU CAKE!
"Don't even mention it!" Bear cried.

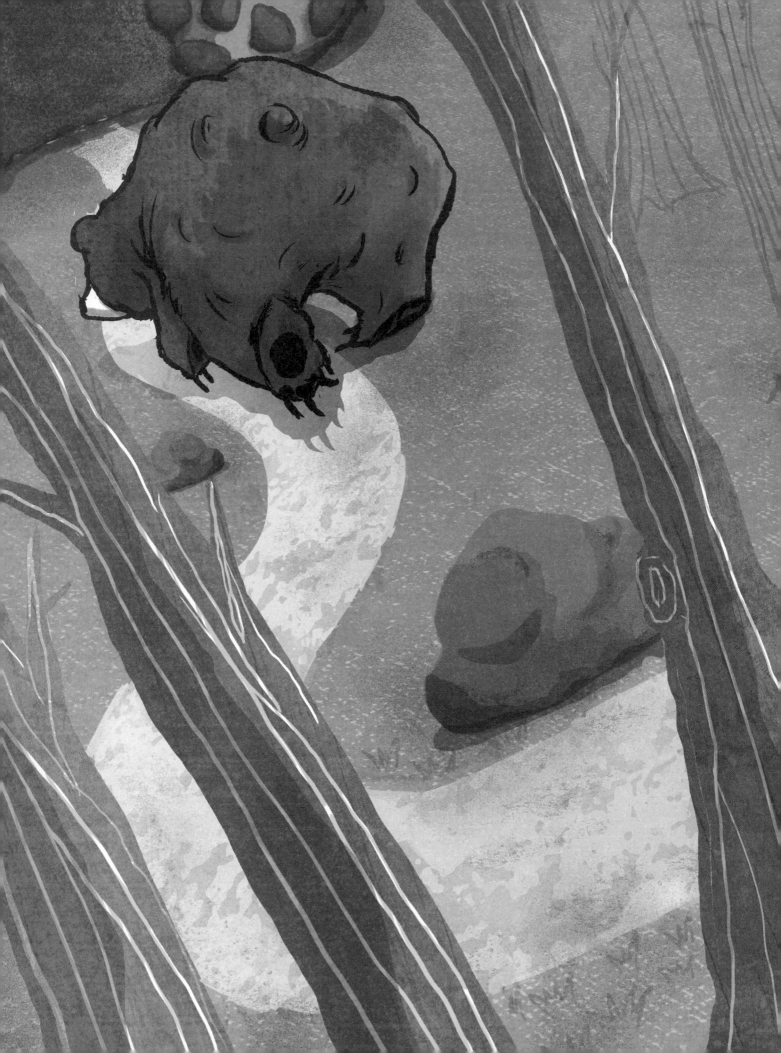

Bear ran to his cave to hide.
Mouse had an idea.
Fox, Snake, and Spider had the same idea.
They all rushed back to Mouse's house . . .

BEWARE OF BEAR

and returned with their manju cakes...
which they tossed, pitched, headed,

and volleyed into Bear's cave.

Then they waited

and waited

and waited

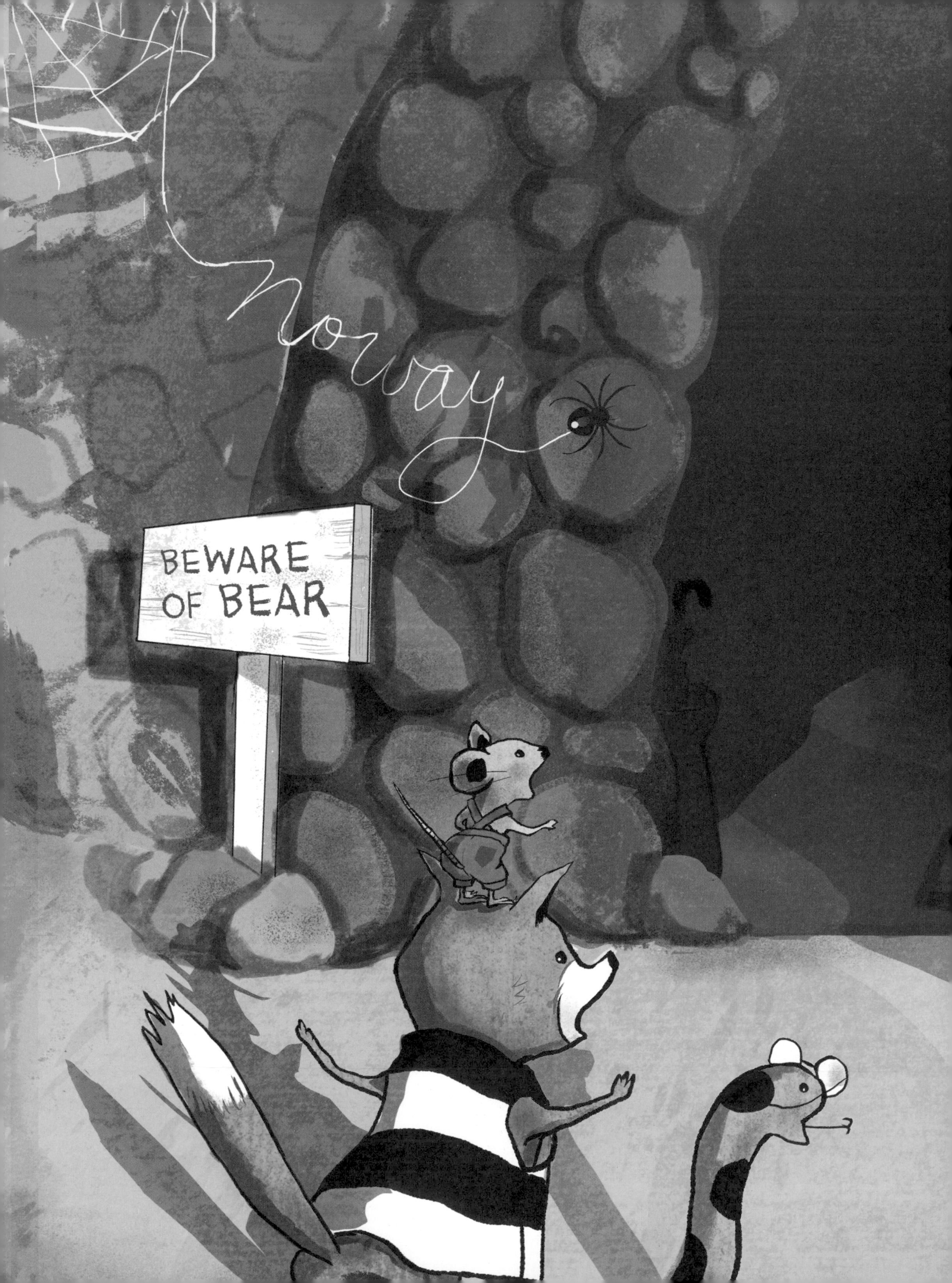
no way
BEWARE
OF BEAR

Bear came out grinning
and licking his lips.

"It's scary how much
I love manju cake,"
said Bear.

## Author's Note

*Let's Scare Bear* is based on a classical *rakugo* story "*Manju Kowai*," which means "Scared of Buns." Rakugo is a traditional verbal entertainment performed onstage by a storyteller. *Manju* is a steamed bun that typically has a sweet filling, such as red bean paste.